The Hex Hunt

Part One

by

Michelle Lowe

Story & illustrations by Michelle Lowe

Editing by Kate Hallman

CONTENTS

To my daughters, Mia & Kirsten

In life, we all take unexpected journeys.

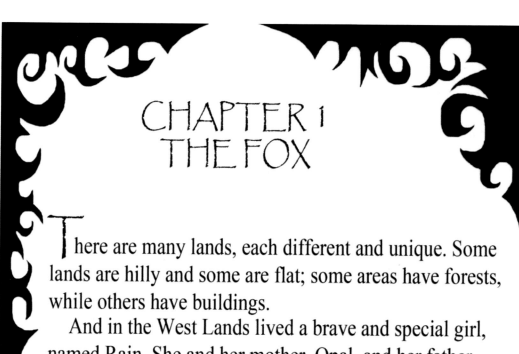

CHAPTER 1
THE FOX

There are many lands, each different and unique. Some lands are hilly and some are flat; some areas have forests, while others have buildings.

And in the West Lands lived a brave and special girl, named Rain. She and her mother, Opal, and her father, Desert, lived in a small cottage out in the countryside.

Their livelihood depended on the crafts they made. They made everything from toys to furniture, wagons to household decorative items. Opal and Desert had even built their cottage before Rain was born.

Rain enjoyed drawing and painting her favorite animal, the fox. Lately, she'd accumulated an audience; a large bird that watched her as she painted.

Rain had many chores, one of which was taking care of the family pony, Raspberry. One morning, as she was grooming Raspberry, Rain noticed a fox sitting on the fence, watching her.

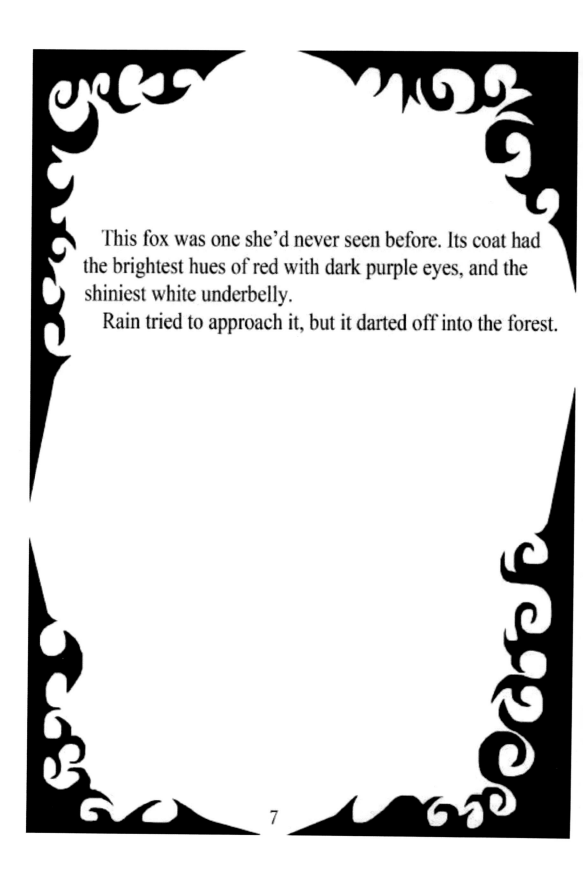

This fox was one she'd never seen before. Its coat had the brightest hues of red with dark purple eyes, and the shiniest white underbelly.

Rain tried to approach it, but it darted off into the forest.

The following day, Opal and Desert packed up their wagon, ready to sell their crafts at the town's annual Starshine Arts & Crafts fair. Usually Rain went with them, but this time she asked to stay behind and in exchange she'd keep the cottage neat and the fruit garden well tended.

After some consideration, Opal and Desert decided that their daughter was old enough to stay by herself. They kissed her goodbye and headed on without her.

In truth, Rain wanted to find the fox. To her surprise though, the fox came to *her!*

'Hello,' said the fox in a young girl's voice.

Rain lost her own voice. *'Did she just talk to me, or have I gone mad?'*

'No,' said the fox without moving her mouth. *'Your mind is perfectly sound. My name is Sage. What is your name?'*

"I'm Rain. How is it that you're talking?"

'I do not speak. I am using telepathy, meaning I can speak to you using only my mind. Animals cannot actually talk, even if they are magical.'

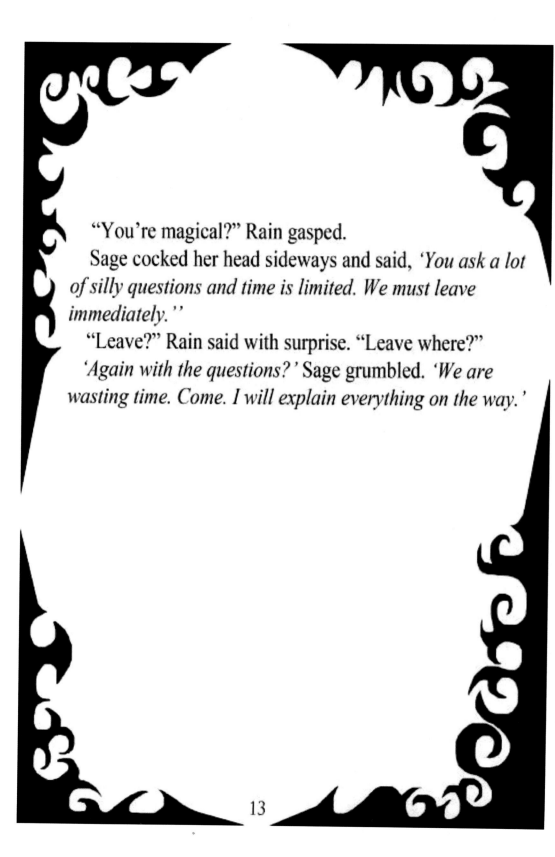

"You're magical?" Rain gasped.

Sage cocked her head sideways and said, *'You ask a lot of silly questions and time is limited. We must leave immediately.''*

"Leave?" Rain said with surprise. "Leave where?"

'Again with the questions?' Sage grumbled. *'We are wasting time. Come. I will explain everything on the way.'*

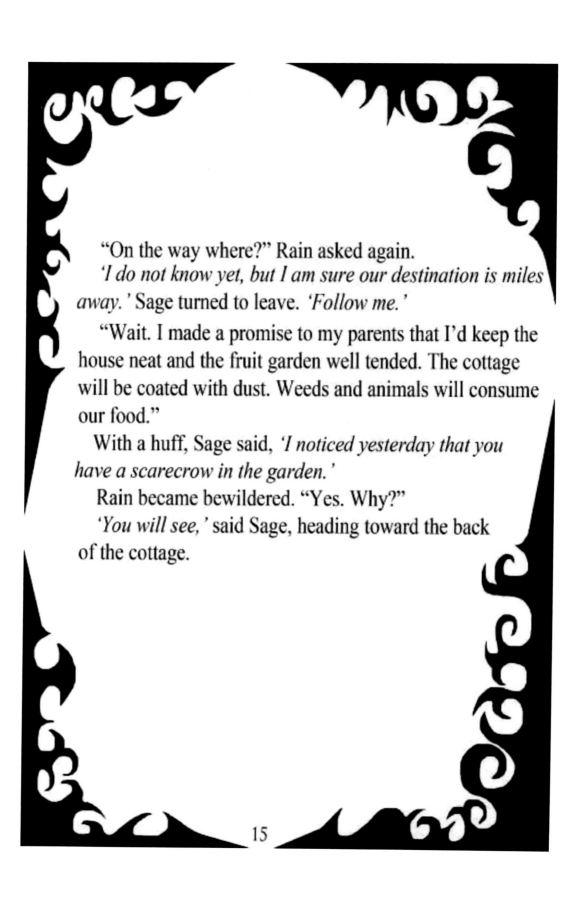

"On the way where?" Rain asked again.

'I do not know yet, but I am sure our destination is miles away.' Sage turned to leave. *'Follow me.'*

"Wait. I made a promise to my parents that I'd keep the house neat and the fruit garden well tended. The cottage will be coated with dust. Weeds and animals will consume our food."

With a huff, Sage said, *'I noticed yesterday that you have a scarecrow in the garden.'*

Rain became bewildered. "Yes. Why?"

'You will see,' said Sage, heading toward the back of the cottage.

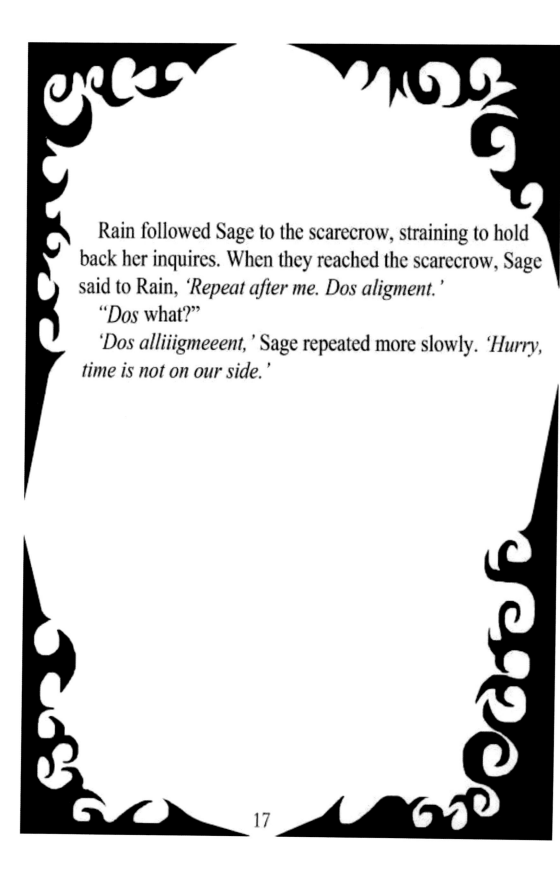

Rain followed Sage to the scarecrow, straining to hold back her inquires. When they reached the scarecrow, Sage said to Rain, *'Repeat after me. Dos aligment.'*

"*Dos* what?"

'Dos alliiigmeeent,' Sage repeated more slowly. *'Hurry, time is not on our side.'*

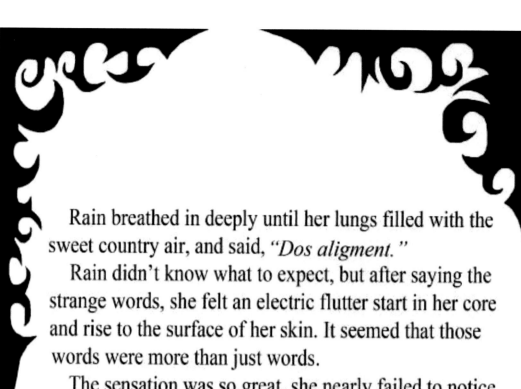

Rain breathed in deeply until her lungs filled with the sweet country air, and said, *"Dos aligment."*

Rain didn't know what to expect, but after saying the strange words, she felt an electric flutter start in her core and rise to the surface of her skin. It seemed that those words were more than just words.

The sensation was so great, she nearly failed to notice the scarecrow freeing itself from its post. Once down, it stumbled a bit on its wobbly straw legs, before hurrying inside the cottage.

Rain was mystified.

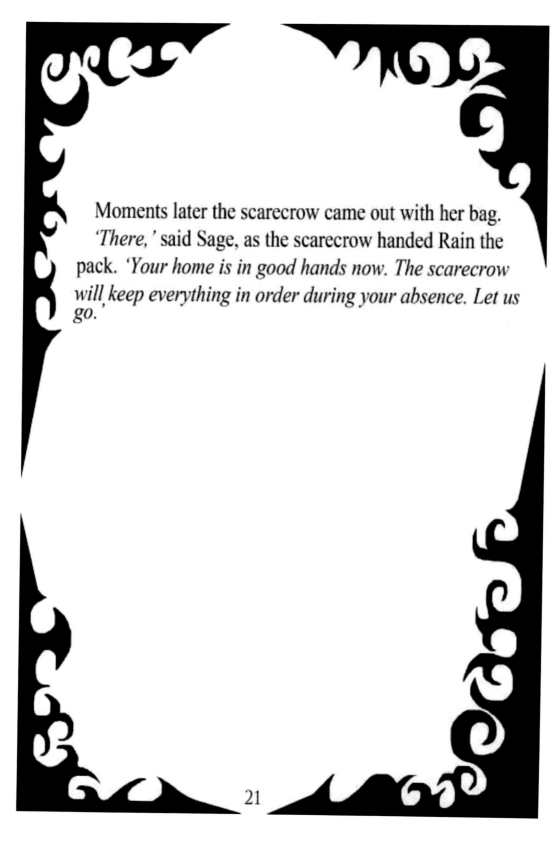

Moments later the scarecrow came out with her bag.

'There,' said Sage, as the scarecrow handed Rain the pack. *'Your home is in good hands now. The scarecrow will keep everything in order during your absence. Let us go.'*

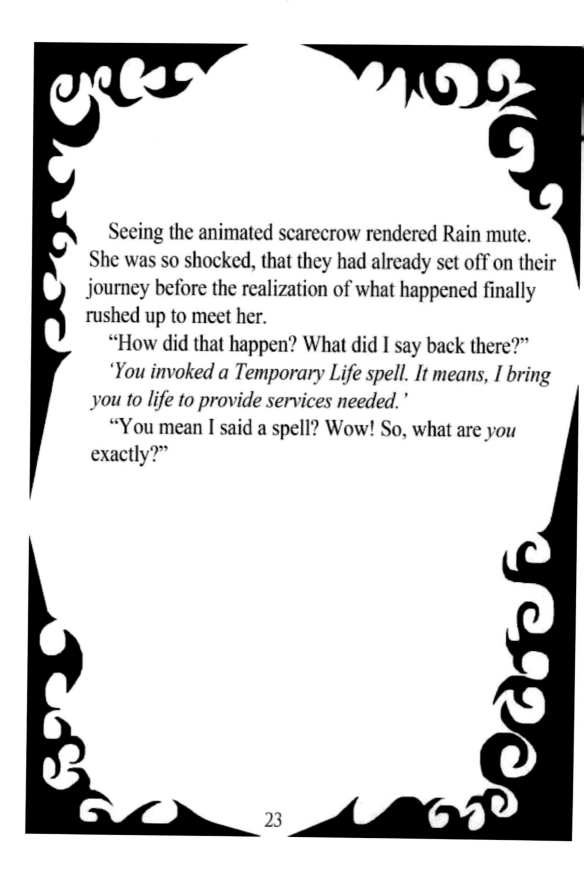

Seeing the animated scarecrow rendered Rain mute. She was so shocked, that they had already set off on their journey before the realization of what happened finally rushed up to meet her.

"How did that happen? What did I say back there?"

'You invoked a Temporary Life spell. It means, I bring you to life to provide services needed.'

"You mean I said a spell? Wow! So, what are *you* exactly?"

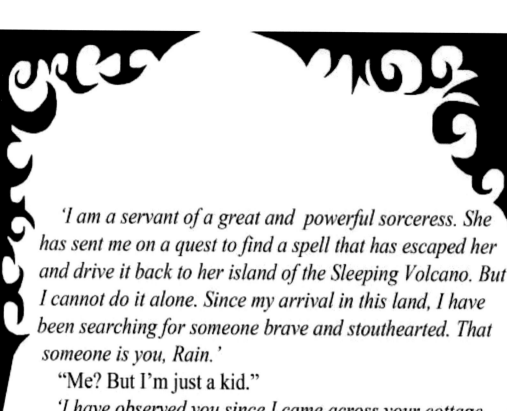

'I am a servant of a great and powerful sorceress. She has sent me on a quest to find a spell that has escaped her and drive it back to her island of the Sleeping Volcano. But I cannot do it alone. Since my arrival in this land, I have been searching for someone brave and stouthearted. That someone is you, Rain.'

"Me? But I'm just a kid."

'I have observed you since I came across your cottage yesterday. I sensed the strength and courage within you.'

"What does the servant of a powerful sorceress need from me? What is this spell we are chasing?"

'My master was working on a protective spell, one meant to keep her safe in the face of adversity. But the spell turned against her instead, creating mischief on her home island. It had gone from being a protective spell to a curse, or hex, if you will.'

"So, why do you need my help?"

'Before the hex escaped, my master developed a spell code written in the Language of Magic. This spell code keeps the hex anchored in one place of its choosing. Otherwise, the hex would continue to drift from one place to another, causing chaos for many. The spell code was also designed to pull the hex back toward the island of the Sleeping Volcano every time it was read aloud.'

"Aloud? Is that what you need from me? To read off this spell code?"

'Yes. As I said, animals, even magical ones, cannot physically speak. I need your voice to actually say the spell code aloud or it will not work.'

"If you can't speak, how can you use umm...tel...tel..."

'Use telepathy,' Sage cut in. *'Because my master created me this way.'*

"Created?" Rain pounced on the word. "You mean you're not real?"

'I am real!' Sage retorted. *'I just was not brought into the world the same way as most living things.'*

"I...I didn't mean anything by that," Rain tried to explain. "I...,"

'We are wasting time,' Sage snapped, moving on. Rain felt bad for what she said, and as they continued on, the two remained silent.

They journeyed a long, long way through The Twisted Forest...

....over the wide Ostrich Plains where ostriches ran wild....

....until crossing Stony Bridge that led into Long Cave which cut straight through Fire Mountain.

Inside Long Cave were thousands of firestones,
illuminating the tunnel in a radiant amber glow.

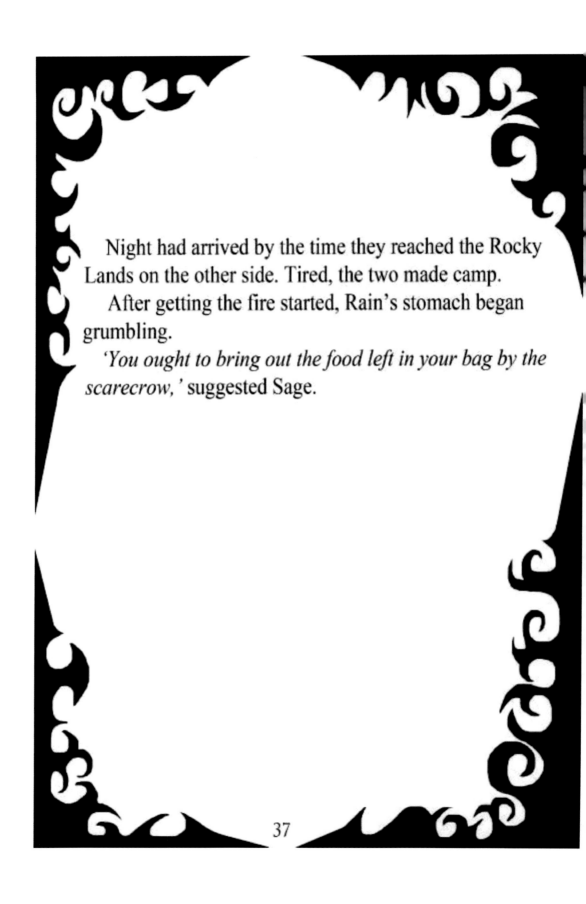

Night had arrived by the time they reached the Rocky Lands on the other side. Tired, the two made camp.

After getting the fire started, Rain's stomach began grumbling.

'You ought to bring out the food left in your bag by the scarecrow,' suggested Sage.

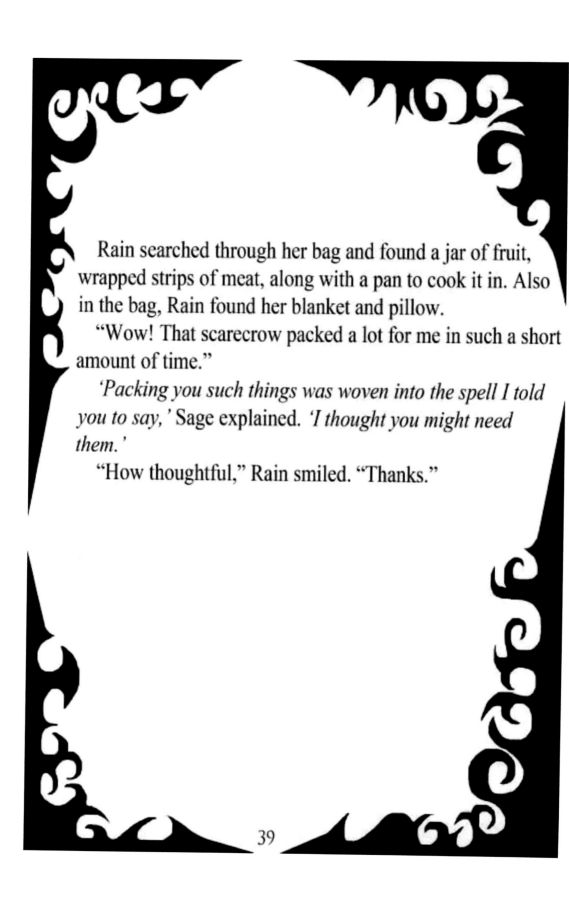

Rain searched through her bag and found a jar of fruit, wrapped strips of meat, along with a pan to cook it in. Also in the bag, Rain found her blanket and pillow.

"Wow! That scarecrow packed a lot for me in such a short amount of time."

'Packing you such things was woven into the spell I told you to say,' Sage explained. *'I thought you might need them.'*

"How thoughtful," Rain smiled. "Thanks."

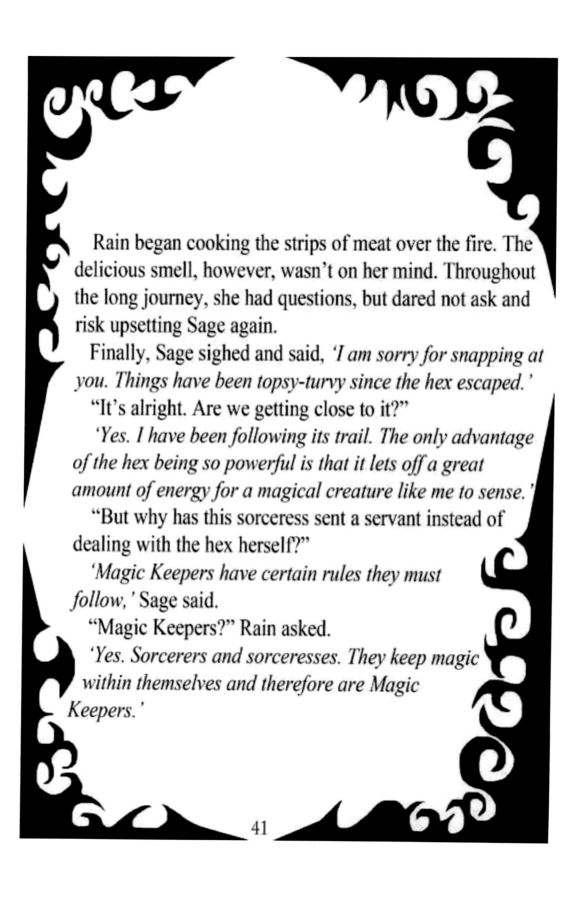

Rain began cooking the strips of meat over the fire. The delicious smell, however, wasn't on her mind. Throughout the long journey, she had questions, but dared not ask and risk upsetting Sage again.

Finally, Sage sighed and said, *'I am sorry for snapping at you. Things have been topsy-turvy since the hex escaped.'*

"It's alright. Are we getting close to it?"

'Yes. I have been following its trail. The only advantage of the hex being so powerful is that it lets off a great amount of energy for a magical creature like me to sense.'

"But why has this sorceress sent a servant instead of dealing with the hex herself?"

'Magic Keepers have certain rules they must follow,' Sage said.

"Magic Keepers?" Rain asked.

'Yes. Sorcerers and sorceresses. They keep magic within themselves and therefore are Magic Keepers.'

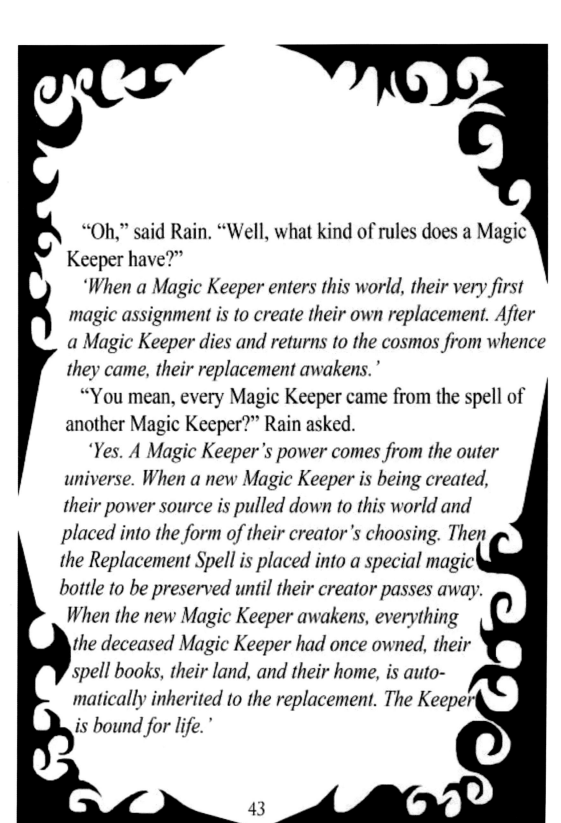

"Oh," said Rain. "Well, what kind of rules does a Magic Keeper have?"

'When a Magic Keeper enters this world, their very first magic assignment is to create their own replacement. After a Magic Keeper dies and returns to the cosmos from whence they came, their replacement awakens.'

"You mean, every Magic Keeper came from the spell of another Magic Keeper?" Rain asked.

'Yes. A Magic Keeper's power comes from the outer universe. When a new Magic Keeper is being created, their power source is pulled down to this world and placed into the form of their creator's choosing. Then the Replacement Spell is placed into a special magic bottle to be preserved until their creator passes away. When the new Magic Keeper awakens, everything the deceased Magic Keeper had once owned, their spell books, their land, and their home, is automatically inherited to the replacement. The Keeper is bound for life.'

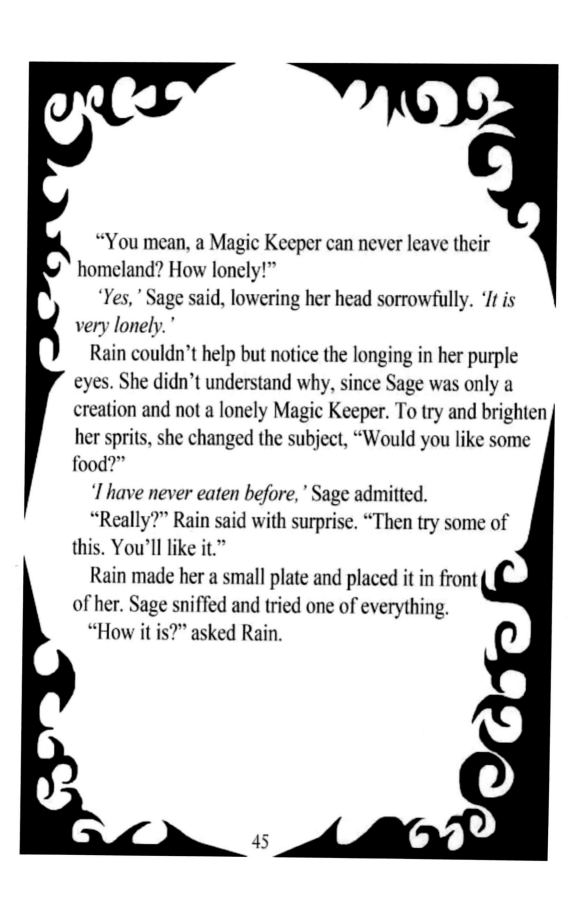

"You mean, a Magic Keeper can never leave their homeland? How lonely!"

'Yes,' Sage said, lowering her head sorrowfully. *'It is very lonely.'*

Rain couldn't help but notice the longing in her purple eyes. She didn't understand why, since Sage was only a creation and not a lonely Magic Keeper. To try and brighten her sprits, she changed the subject, "Would you like some food?"

'I have never eaten before,' Sage admitted.

"Really?" Rain said with surprise. "Then try some of this. You'll like it."

Rain made her a small plate and placed it in front of her. Sage sniffed and tried one of everything.

"How it is?" asked Rain.

Sage flashed a big smile. *'Yum!'*

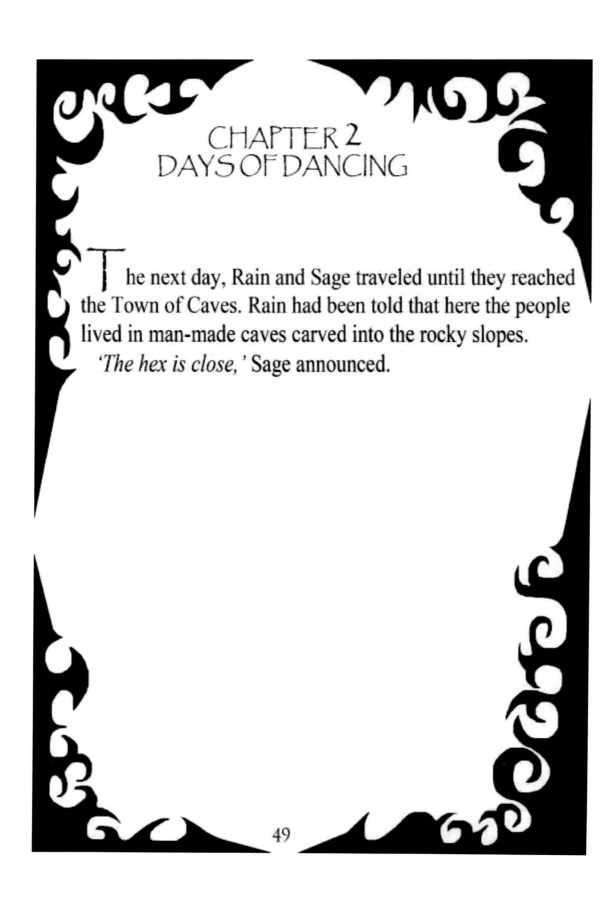

CHAPTER 2
DAYS OF DANCING

The next day, Rain and Sage traveled until they reached the Town of Caves. Rain had been told that here the people lived in man-made caves carved into the rocky slopes.

'*The hex is close,*' Sage announced.

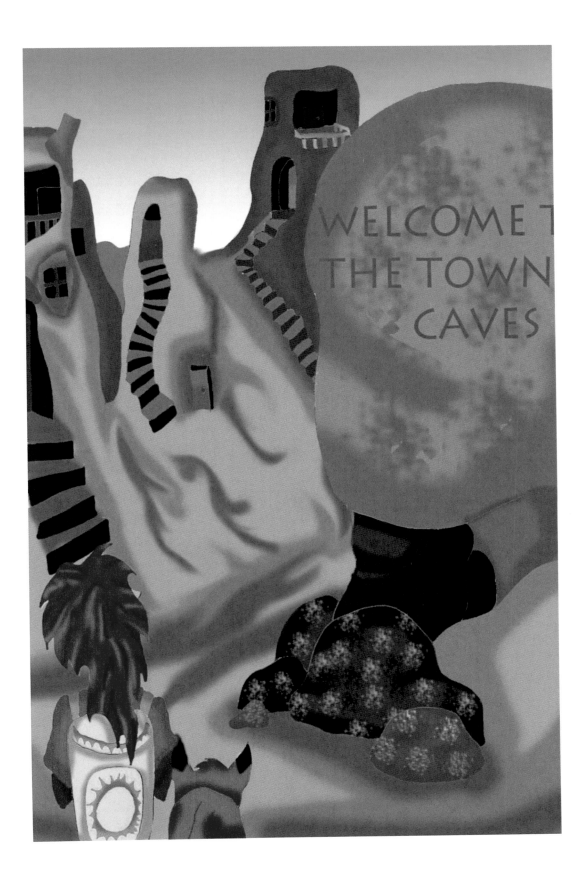

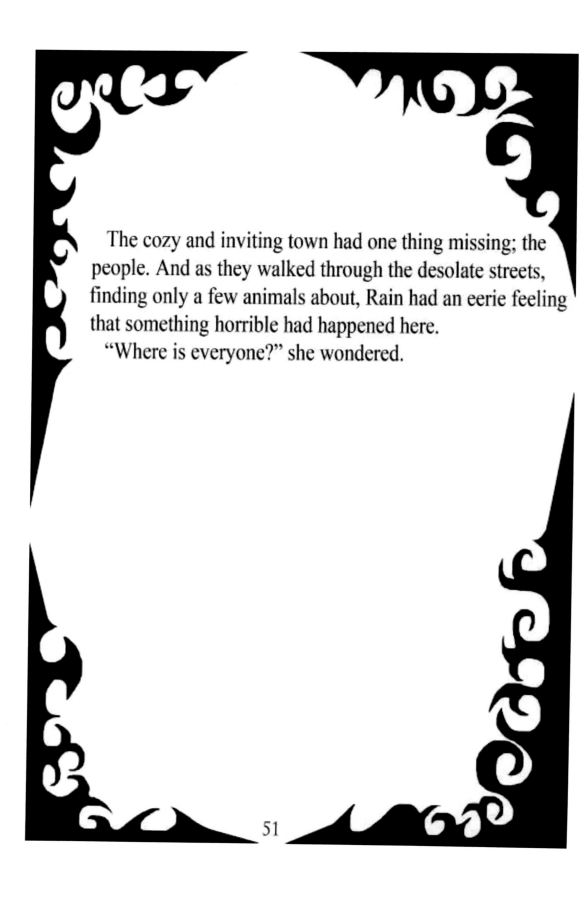

The cozy and inviting town had one thing missing; the people. And as they walked through the desolate streets, finding only a few animals about, Rain had an eerie feeling that something horrible had happened here.

"Where is everyone?" she wondered.

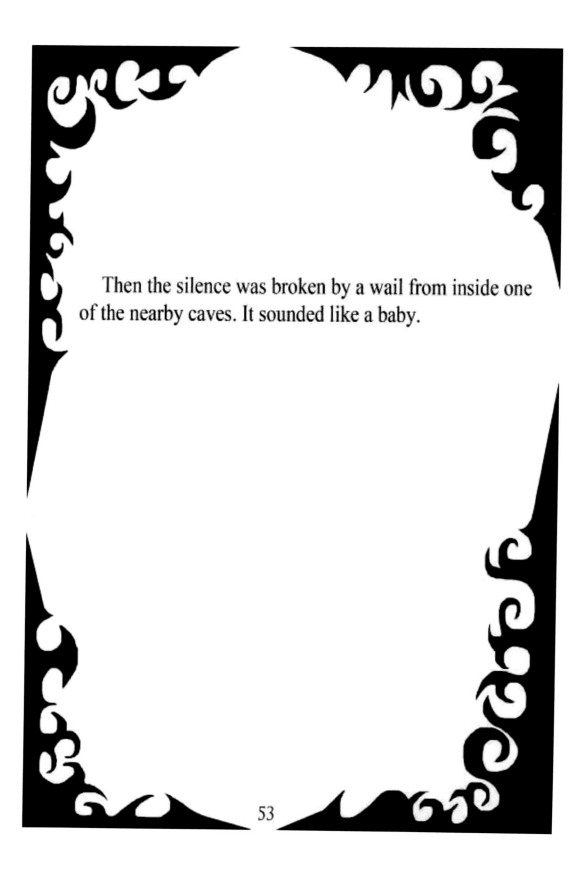

Then the silence was broken by a wail from inside one of the nearby caves. It sounded like a baby.

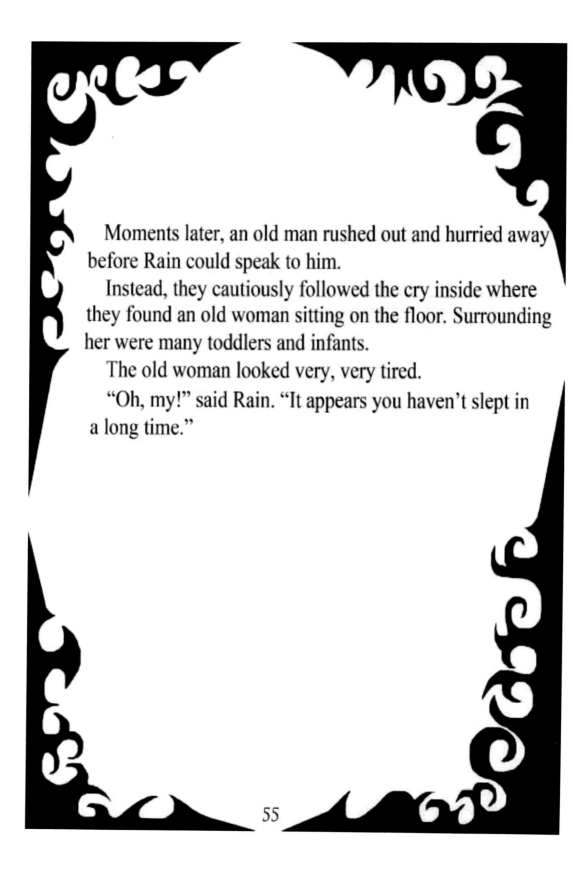

Moments later, an old man rushed out and hurried away before Rain could speak to him.

Instead, they cautiously followed the cry inside where they found an old woman sitting on the floor. Surrounding her were many toddlers and infants.

The old woman looked very, very tired.

"Oh, my!" said Rain. "It appears you haven't slept in a long time."

"That's because I haven't, my dear," the old woman groaned. "My husband and I have been watching over all these little ones for days now."

"Why? Where are their parents?"

"Gone!" the old woman said. "My husband and I came into town with crops to sell, and everyone, save for these little ones, had vanished!"

The old woman truly looked tired, indeed. Dark circles had bloomed around her faded eyes and she spoke in an exasperated whisper. "We found one toddler wandering the street while my husband and I searched for the people. Eventually, we came across other hungry and weeping children."

Sage's ears perked up. *'The hex took the towns-people away. We find them, we find the hex.'*

"We aren't able to fetch help," the old woman continued. "The next town is so far away and we're too old to travel with all these babies. Oh, Mr. Cod, what have you done?"

"Sorry?" Rain inquired. "Who's Mr. Cod?"

"He's a wealthy hermit living alone in his château," came the voice of the old man, carrying in changing wipes and bottles of milk. "I went there for help, but I didn't step one foot onto his property when I saw a dark cloud hovering over his entire estate. I suspected something strange happening inside the château, so I left as fast as my feet could carry me!"

"Where is this château?" Rain asked.

"Follow the road that cuts through the rocky slopes. You can't miss it."

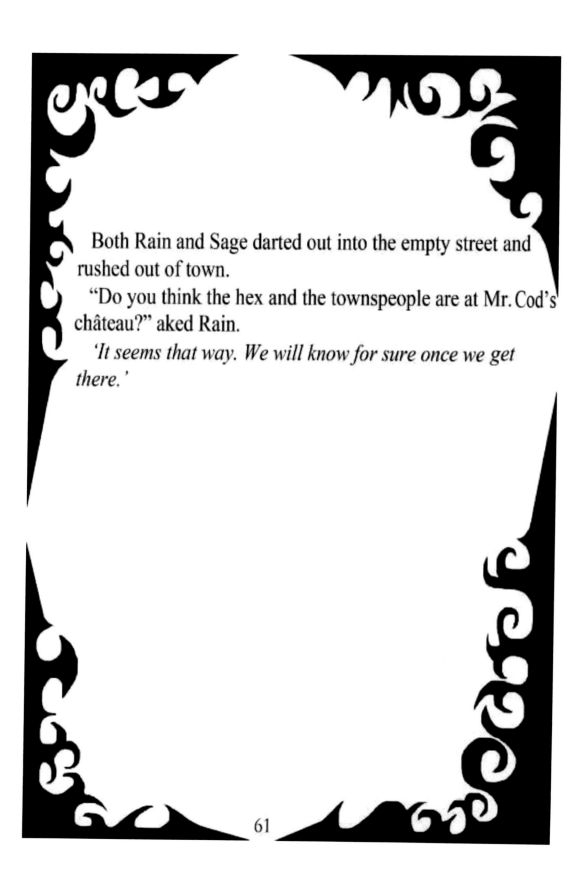

Both Rain and Sage darted out into the empty street and rushed out of town.

"Do you think the hex and the townspeople are at Mr. Cod's château?" aked Rain.

'It seems that way. We will know for sure once we get there.'

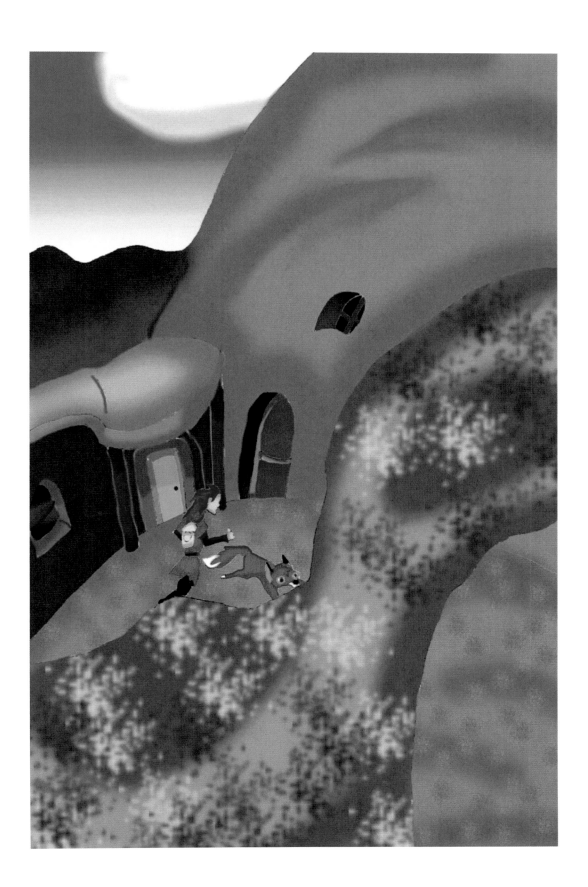

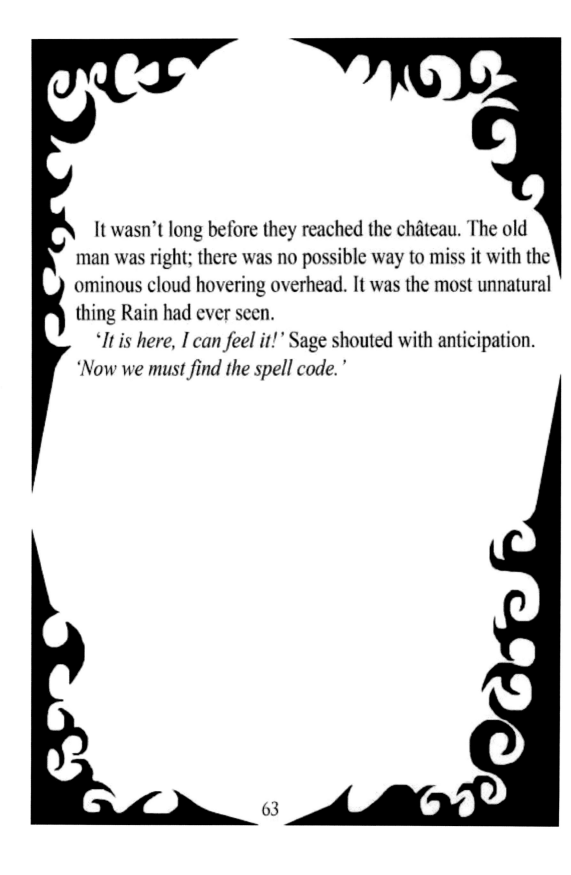

It wasn't long before they reached the château. The old man was right; there was no possible way to miss it with the ominous cloud hovering overhead. It was the most unnatural thing Rain had ever seen.

'*It is here, I can feel it!*' Sage shouted with anticipation. '*Now we must find the spell code.*'

Rain became nervous as they crept to a window near the back. The whole area within the cloud's shadow felt cold and unforgiving. It made Rain shiver. Sage peered in through one window and said, *'Rain, look!'*

Rain looked in and gasped with amazement.

Inside, in what seemed like a ballroom, people were moving about in a bizarre trance-like dance.

"Why are they dancing?"

'They are under the hex's control,' Sage explained grimly. *'Since it is stuck here, it seeks entertainment. It must have put these people in a trance, forcing them to leave their homes to come here. They do not even realize they have been dancing for days.'*

"How do you know they've been dancing for days?"

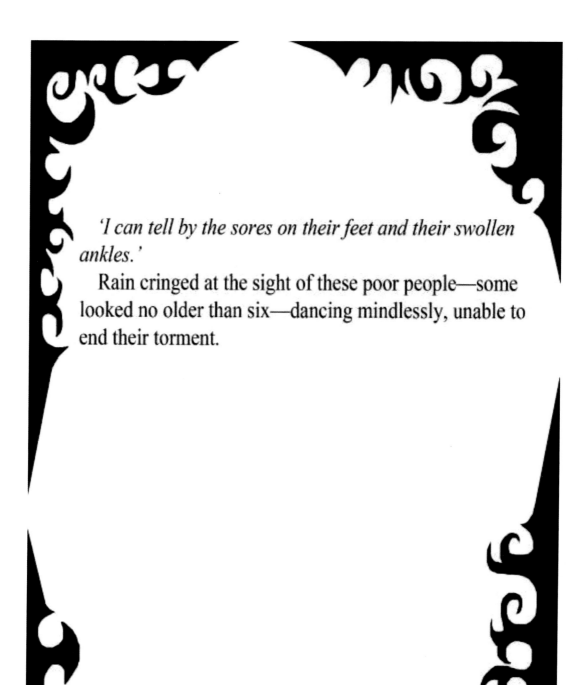

'I can tell by the sores on their feet and their swollen ankles.'

Rain cringed at the sight of these poor people—some looked no older than six—dancing mindlessly, unable to end their torment.

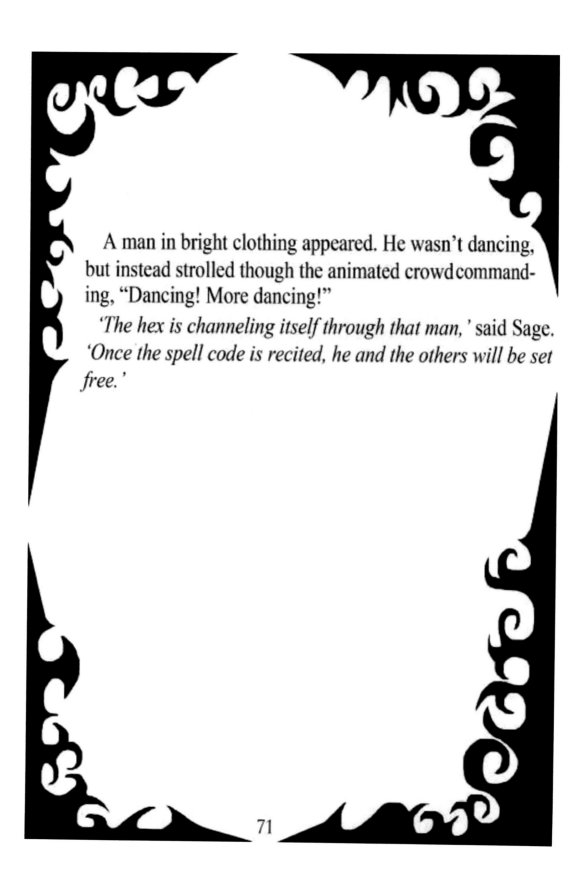

A man in bright clothing appeared. He wasn't dancing, but instead strolled though the animated crowd commanding, "Dancing! More dancing!"

'The hex is channeling itself through that man,' said Sage. 'Once the spell code is recited, he and the others will be set free.'

Without a moment's hesitation, they searched around the château. They found a cellar door on the other side and descended down the steps.

The darkness was thick inside the cellar.

"I can't see," Rain complained.

'*Repeat after me,*' said Sage. '*Esk toknox.*'

Rain took a breath and said, *"Esk toknox."*

A light appeared before her. It startled her so much, she almost failed to notice another magical charge fluttering within her.

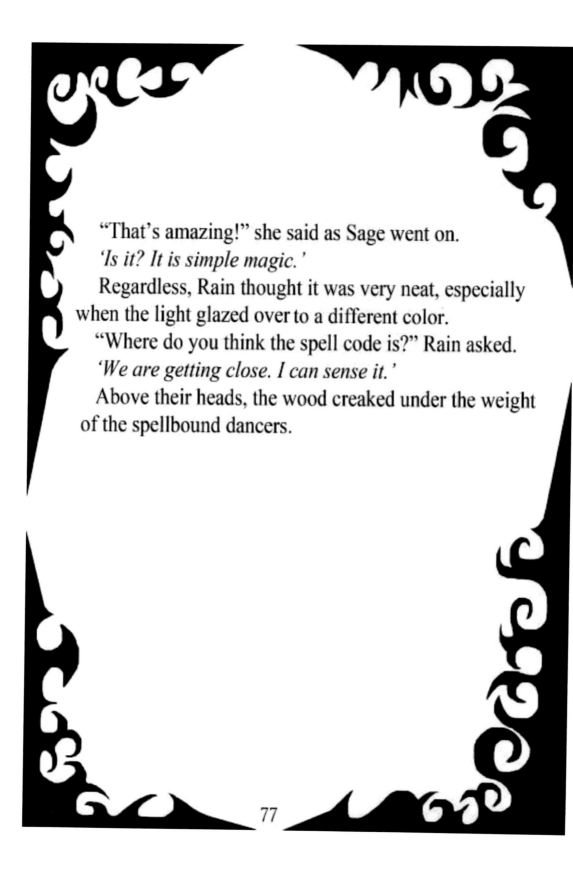

"That's amazing!" she said as Sage went on.

'Is it? It is simple magic.'

Regardless, Rain thought it was very neat, especially when the light glazed over to a different color.

"Where do you think the spell code is?" Rain asked.

'We are getting close. I can sense it.'

Above their heads, the wood creaked under the weight of the spellbound dancers.

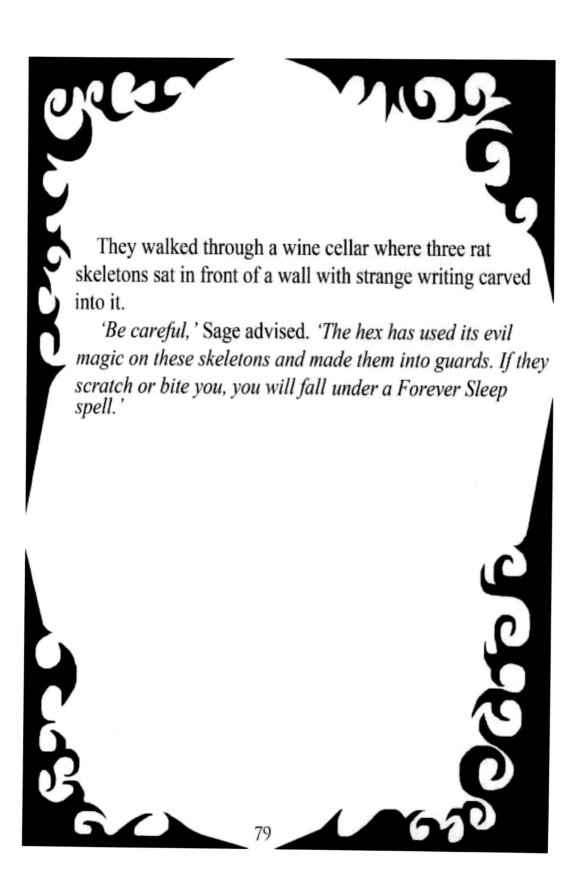

They walked through a wine cellar where three rat skeletons sat in front of a wall with strange writing carved into it.

'Be careful,' Sage advised. 'The hex has used its evil magic on these skeletons and made them into guards. If they scratch or bite you, you will fall under a Forever Sleep spell.'

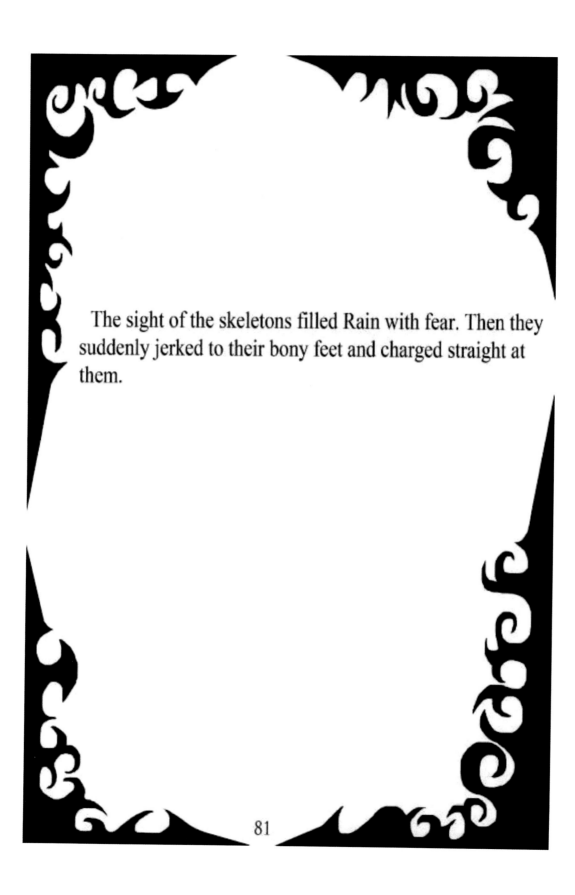

The sight of the skeletons filled Rain with fear. Then they suddenly jerked to their bony feet and charged straight at them.

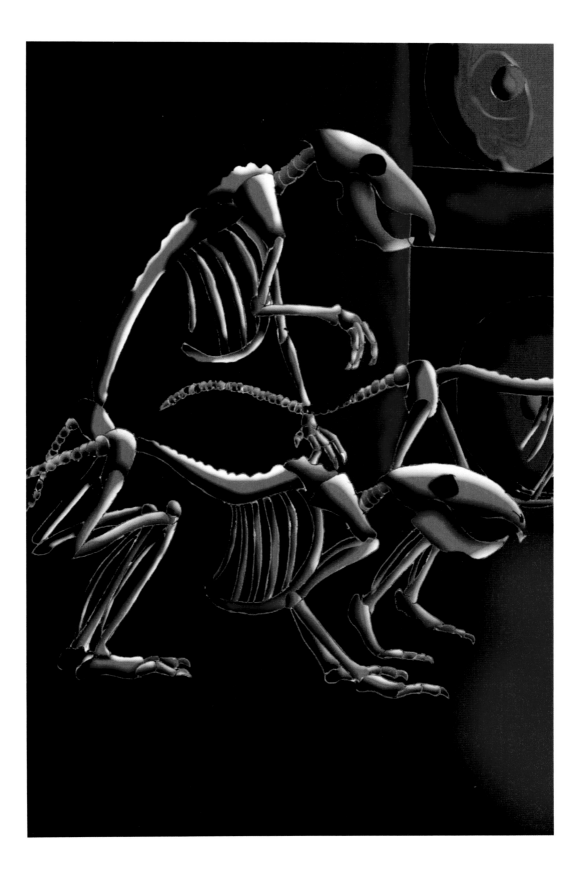

'*Quick! Say lockperie!*' Sage ordered.

Rain's fear had blocked out her words as the rat skeletons leaped into the air toward her.

'*Say it!*' Sage commanded.

Rain shut her eyes tight and shouted, "*Lockperie!*"

A few seconds later, she opened her eyes to see the skeletons suspended in midair only inches from her.

'*Now* that *is amazing,*' said Sage, '*because I was not sure if that was the right spell.*'

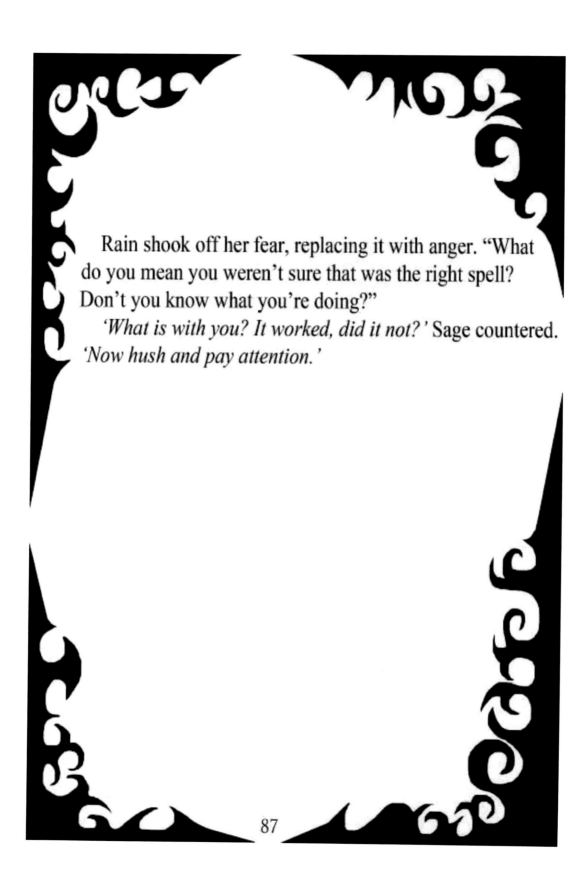

Rain shook off her fear, replacing it with anger. "What do you mean you weren't sure that was the right spell? Don't you know what you're doing?"

'What is with you? It worked, did it not?' Sage countered. *'Now hush and pay attention.'*

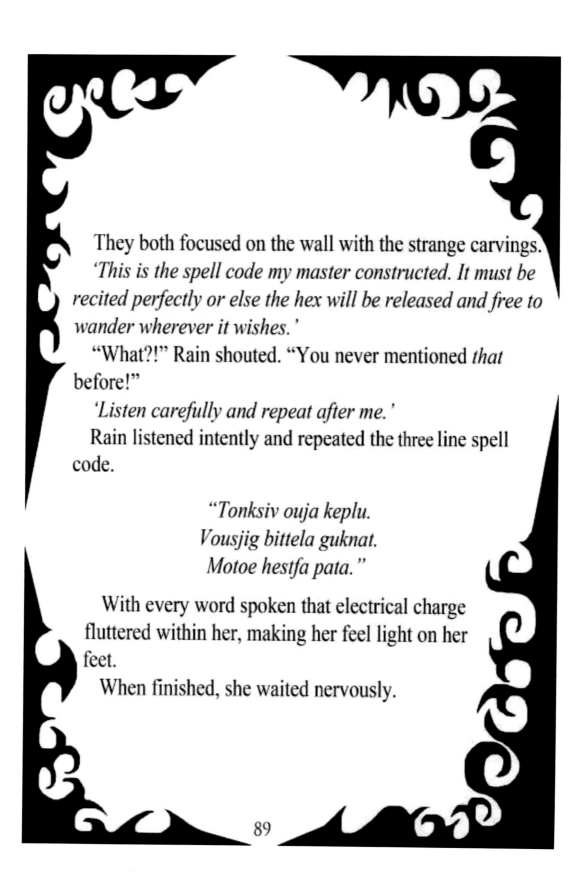

They both focused on the wall with the strange carvings.

'This is the spell code my master constructed. It must be recited perfectly or else the hex will be released and free to wander wherever it wishes.'

"What?!" Rain shouted. "You never mentioned *that* before!"

'Listen carefully and repeat after me.'

Rain listened intently and repeated the three line spell code.

> *"Tonksiv ouja keplu.*
> *Vousjig bittela guknat.*
> *Motoe hestfa pata."*

With every word spoken that electrical charge fluttered within her, making her feel light on her feet.

When finished, she waited nervously.

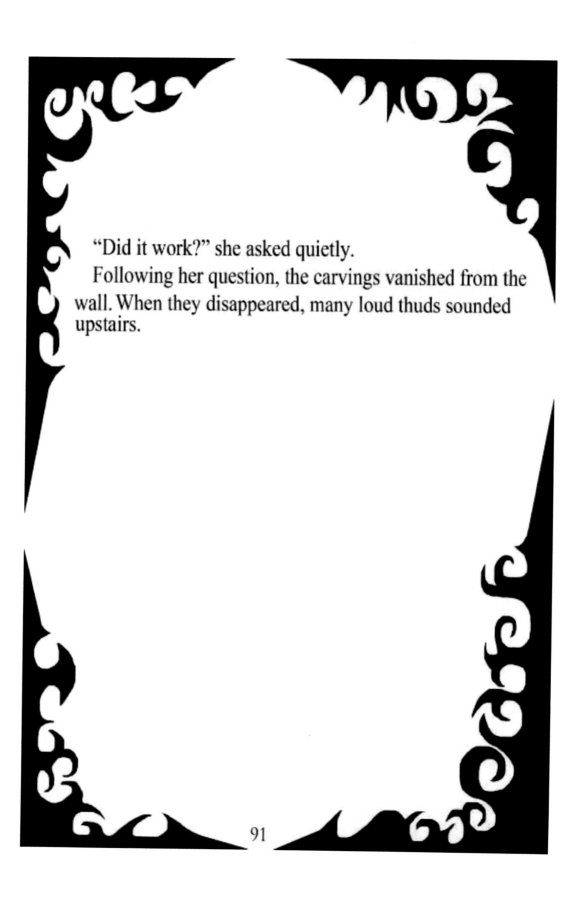

"Did it work?" she asked quietly.

Following her question, the carvings vanished from the wall. When they disappeared, many loud thuds sounded upstairs.

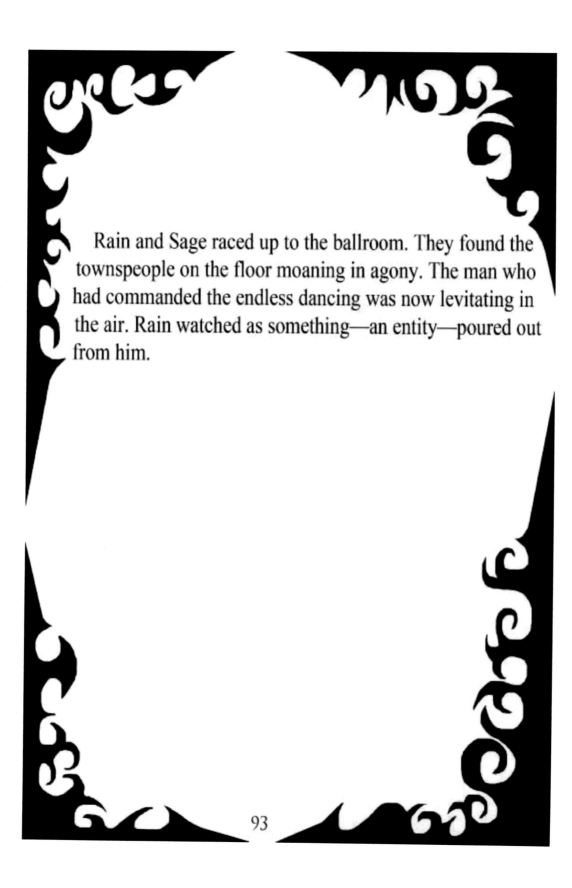

Rain and Sage raced up to the ballroom. They found the townspeople on the floor moaning in agony. The man who had commanded the endless dancing was now levitating in the air. Rain watched as something—an entity—poured out from him.

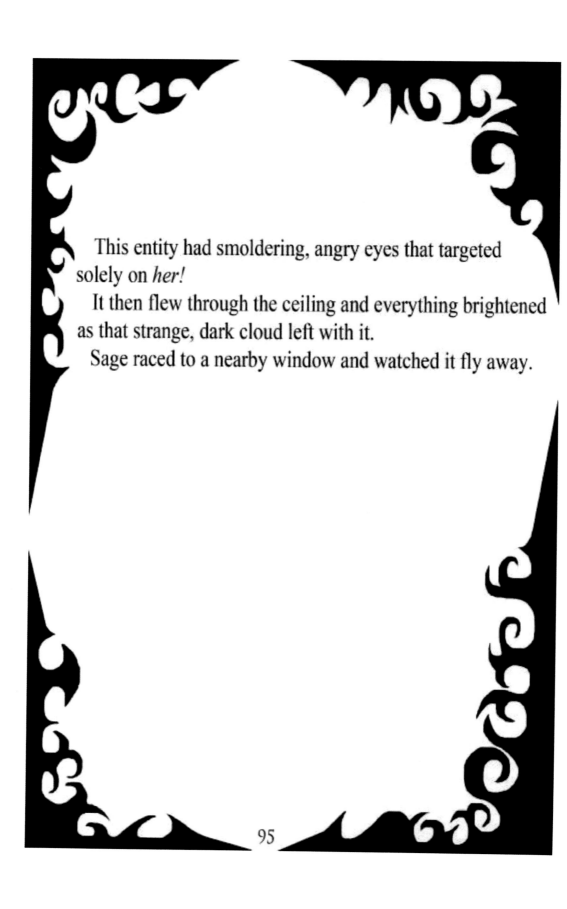

This entity had smoldering, angry eyes that targeted solely on *her!*

It then flew through the ceiling and everything brightened as that strange, dark cloud left with it.

Sage raced to a nearby window and watched it fly away.

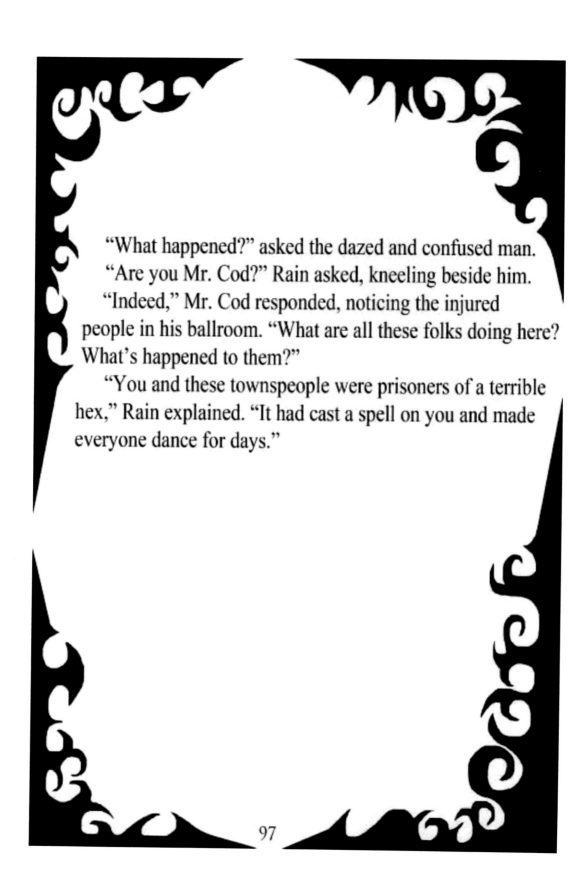

"What happened?" asked the dazed and confused man.

"Are you Mr. Cod?" Rain asked, kneeling beside him.

"Indeed," Mr. Cod responded, noticing the injured people in his ballroom. "What are all these folks doing here? What's happened to them?"

"You and these townspeople were prisoners of a terrible hex," Rain explained. "It had cast a spell on you and made everyone dance for days."

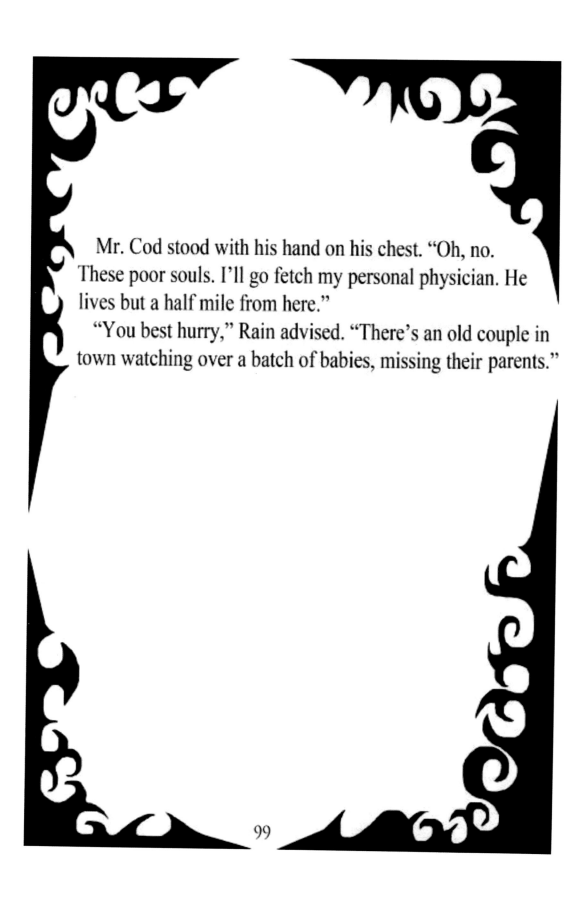

Mr. Cod stood with his hand on his chest. "Oh, no. These poor souls. I'll go fetch my personal physician. He lives but a half mile from here."

"You best hurry," Rain advised. "There's an old couple in town watching over a batch of babies, missing their parents."

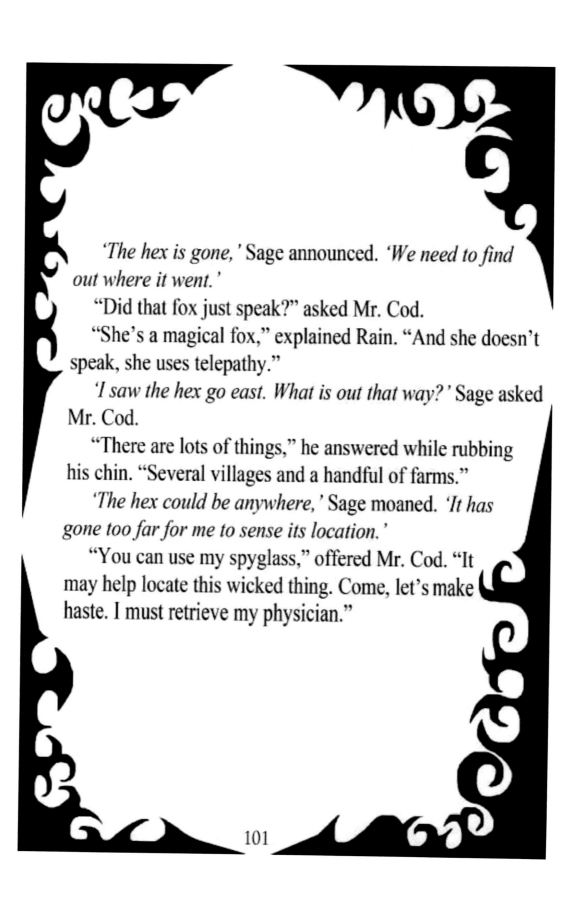

'The hex is gone,' Sage announced. 'We need to find out where it went.'

"Did that fox just speak?" asked Mr. Cod.

"She's a magical fox," explained Rain. "And she doesn't speak, she uses telepathy."

'I saw the hex go east. What is out that way?' Sage asked Mr. Cod.

"There are lots of things," he answered while rubbing his chin. "Several villages and a handful of farms."

'The hex could be anywhere,' Sage moaned. 'It has gone too far for me to sense its location.'

"You can use my spyglass," offered Mr. Cod. "It may help locate this wicked thing. Come, let's make haste. I must retrieve my physician."

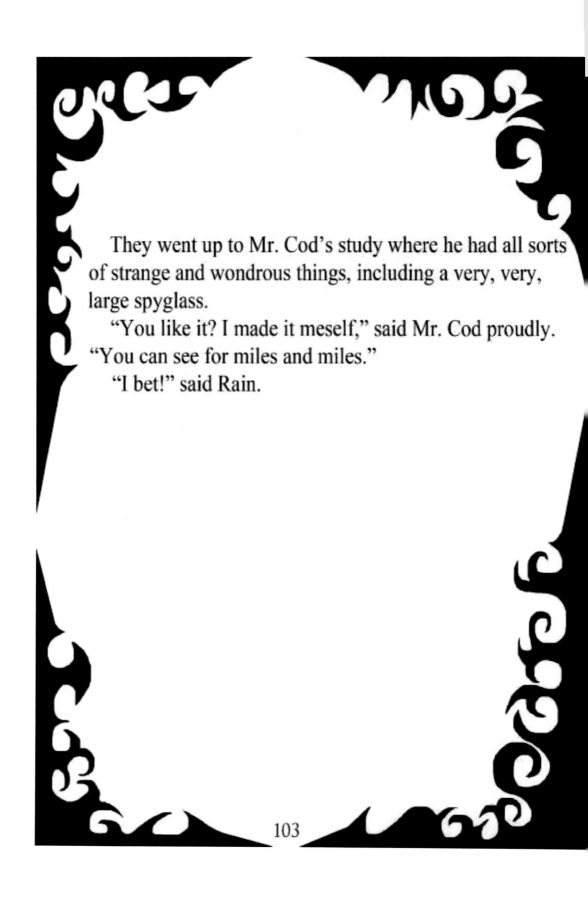

They went up to Mr. Cod's study where he had all sorts of strange and wondrous things, including a very, very, large spyglass.

"You like it? I made it meself," said Mr. Cod proudly. "You can see for miles and miles."

"I bet!" said Rain.

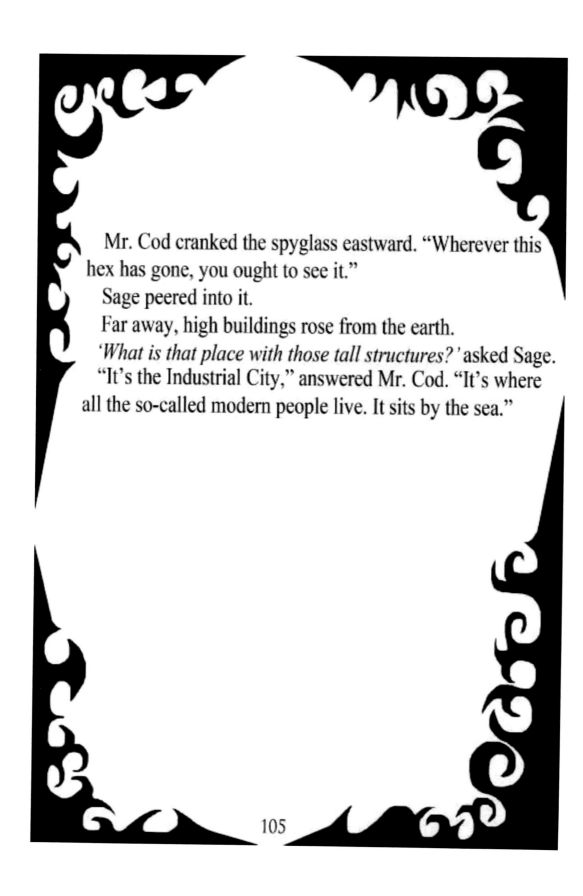

Mr. Cod cranked the spyglass eastward. "Wherever this hex has gone, you ought to see it."

Sage peered into it.

Far away, high buildings rose from the earth.

'What is that place with those tall structures?' asked Sage.

"It's the Industrial City," answered Mr. Cod. "It's where all the so-called modern people live. It sits by the sea."

'*That is where the hex has gone,*' Sage said. '*Come, Rain!*'

Rain, however, was exhausted. She just knew she wouldn't be able to walk another mile, much less many miles! But before she had a chance to say anything to Sage about it, she'd already run out of the room.

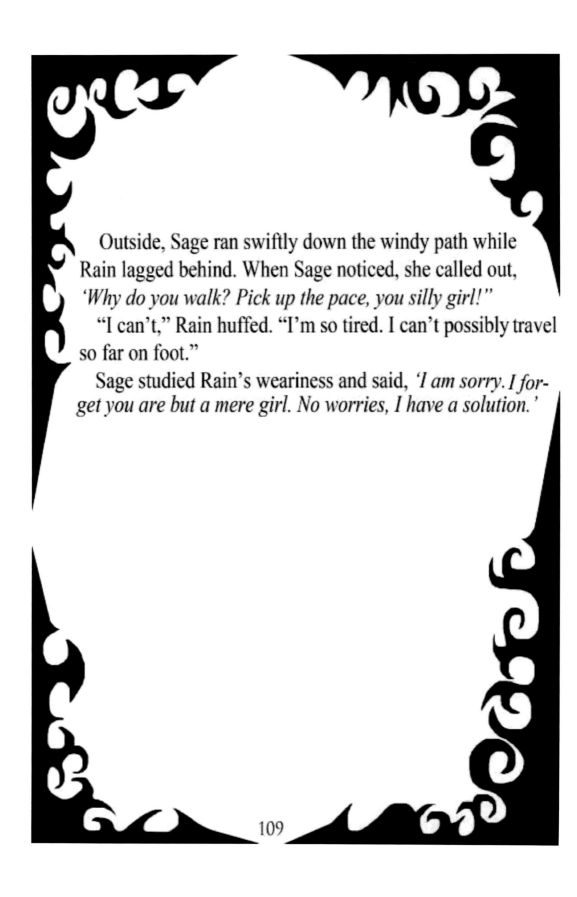

Outside, Sage ran swiftly down the windy path while Rain lagged behind. When Sage noticed, she called out, *'Why do you walk? Pick up the pace, you silly girl!"*

"I can't," Rain huffed. "I'm so tired. I can't possibly travel so far on foot."

Sage studied Rain's weariness and said, *'I am sorry. I forget you are but a mere girl. No worries, I have a solution.'*

Rain then witnessed the most remarkable thing she'd ever seen. Sage leaped high into the air and morphed from being a petite fox into something completely different.

A Clydesdale Pegasus!

"Y…you've turned into a Pegasus?!" Rain stammered.

'I can transform into any animal I wish, or in this case, whatever animal is needed.'

"What do you mean by whatever animal is needed?"

'It was no coincidence that I came to you in the form of a fox. I knew you liked foxes by the drawings and paintings you did.'

"*You* were that bird, weren't you?" said Rain, remembering the large bird that seemed to observe her artwork.

'Yes. I had been in the air when I spotted you drawing in your yard. I transformed into a fox in hopes that you would be more willing to join me. And now that you are in need of a lift and we have to reach the city quickly, I am now a Pegasus.'

"That's amazing!" said Rain, climbing on.

'You think that is amazing as well?' Sage snorted. *'Wow, you are easily entertained! Hang on tight!'*

Rain held onto Sage's long mane just as she flapped her large, colorful wings, and took to the sky.

To Be Continued....

Take a sneak peek at
The Hex Hunt Vol. 2,
Surviving the Sea.

After defeating the hex in Mr. Cod's château, Rain and Sage journey to the Industrial City only to discover, to their horror, that the hex has turned it into a polluted, frightening place.

Fortunately, they meet a helpful young boy named Jayden, who becomes a valued friend.

When they discover the spell code
inside a Mechanical Garden, Rain
reads it and drives the hex far out to sea.

The three find passage on board Captain Natsuko's ship, and think all is well.

However the hex has power greater than they suspect. Halfway through their journey, the hex attacks and attempts to destroy them by resurrecting a dead pirate and his lost vessel, Jupiter, from the bottom of the sea!

Will Rain, Sage, and Jayden escape the power of the hex and be able to continue on with their mission?

Find out in The Hex Hunt: Surviving the Sea.

Coming June, 1st. 2013!

THE HEX HUNT

Surviving the Sea

MICHELLE LOWE

ACKNOWLEDGMENTS

I like to thank the ones who have made this book possible:
Jim & Janice Lowe, Kate Hallman, Jonathan Gold,
Landry Prichard, & most of all my daughters, Mia &
Kirsten, who have inspired me to take this new journey.

ABOUT THE AUTHOR

Michelle Lowe, author of The Warning and Atlantic Pyramid, has written her first children's book, The Hex Hunt.

Michelle was born June 18th, 1979 in Clayton County, Georgia and raised in Peachtree City. In '98 she attended college for graphic design, only to leave to pursue a writing career. Currently, she lives in Irvine, California with husband Ben and daughters, Mia and Kirsten.

For more information, visit the author's website at www.michellelowe.net.

.

Manufactured by Amazon.ca
Bolton, ON

21990860R00093